Jaden Parker

The Baby Is Coming

written by

LaToya D. Thomas & Ollie B. Wheeler III

A Note from the Authors

We hope you are enjoying the Jaden Parker book series. Our books are fun, family-oriented with real-life themes. In each book, we share small but powerful lessons, such as overcoming fear and being kind. In our first book, "The Big Move," Jaden deals with moving to a new town and visiting a new doctor. In this book, he deals with getting a new baby sister. As you read, think about how you might handle these situations and whether Jaden's responses would work for you in your setting.

We encourage you to read each book in the series so that you can follow the life of Jaden Parker. Reading is a gift that allows you to travel to the most unimaginable places in the world. You can travel to places, like Cuddlesburg, where your feet may never trot, but where your mind can frolic and explore. Reading helps you to become wiser, more adventurous, and more apt to deal with challenges. You can become an astronaut, a doctor, a lawyer, a teacher, or whatever you wish; it all begins with the pages of a book.

More Books from the Authors

@jadenparkerbooks

ISBN 978-1-7361491-2-6 (paperback)
      978-1-7361491-3-3 (hardcover)

Published by Wellsprings United

Jaden Parker series
Book 1: The Big Move

Jaden Parker and his growing family recently moved to a new town called Cuddlesburg. Jaden misses his old home, but he is doing his best to adjust to his new town. When Daddy mentions to Jaden that he would have to visit a new doctor, Jaden panics. Doctors give Jaden the heebie-jeebies! Let's venture inside the book to discover how Jaden copes with moving to a new town and visiting his new doctor.

THIS BOOK BELONGS TO

_____

_____

_____

JADEN PARKER BOOKS
Wellsprings United

"The baby is coming! The baby is coming!" Jaden Parker yelled from the top of the treehouse.

It had been several months since the Parker family moved to Cuddlesburg, and everything was going well for Jaden. He had made new friends, built a treehouse with Daddy, and even set up a lemonade stand in his front yard.

Yet nothing excited Jaden more than the upcoming arrival of his baby sister. Everywhere he went, he shared the great news.

Jaden was thrilled when he thought of the wonderful things he would do with Baby Amaya. He dreamed of playing hide-and-seek, camping in the backyard, and eating ice cream with sprinkles. He was also excited to chase her around the house.

Every day, Jaden would whisper to Amaya in Mommy's belly, "We are going to have so much fun."

Mommy would smile and hug Jaden tightly, and then she would whisper back, "You are going to be the best big brother in the world!"

Jaden wanted everything to be special for Amaya, so he helped Daddy paint and decorate the nursery. He even chose the color for the walls— periwinkle blue.

Once the nursery was just about finished, Daddy and Jaden assembled Amaya's crib. Jaden was very careful to follow all the instructions. When they were done, he gently placed a plush pink teddy bear into Amaya's crib.

"You did a great job, champ!" Daddy high-fived Jaden.

"We are a great team, Daddy," said Jaden. "I can't wait until Amaya sees her crib."

"Well, tomorrow is the big day," announced Daddy. "When she comes home, I know she is going to love all the work you did in here."

Moments later, Grandma and Grandpa arrived with big smiles and gifts in hand.

"Look who's here," said Daddy.

"Grandma and Grandpa, yay!" Jaden ran and leaped into Grandpa's arms.

"We have something special for you," announced Grandma.

Grandpa handed Jaden a beautifully wrapped gift. Jaden beamed with joy and quickly opened it.

"A toy truck! I love it. I love it!" Jaden jumped up and down, holding up his new toy.

"Take it easy, champ," said Daddy. "It's time for Mommy and me to head to the hospital."

Daddy picked up the bag that had been sitting near the front door.

Mommy gave Jaden a big hug. "Remember to be a good listener for Grandma and Grandpa. Okay, honey?"

"I promise, Mommy. And when you come home, I'll get to meet Amaya?"

"That's right, honey, and you'll officially be a big brother!"

Jaden could hardly contain his excitement.

"Who wants brownies?" Grandma asked as Grandpa and Jaden scurried to the treehouse.

"I do! I do!" Jaden yelled back loud enough for Grandma to hear.

Grandpa chuckled. "Me too! Me too!"

Grandma went inside to make her famous chocolate fudge brownies while Jaden and Grandpa continued to play outside.

After a while, it was time to go inside to get washed up for dinner.

The next day, Jaden played soccer with Grandpa and two neighborhood friends. He also read books with Grandma and ate more of her delicious chocolate fudge brownies.

As the day went on, Jaden became restless. He missed Mommy and Daddy, and he wanted to have fun with his new baby sister!

That evening, Jaden's parents walked through the front door. Jaden could not believe his eyes. Daddy was carrying baby Amaya in her car seat.

"Amaya! She's here!" Jaden announced. "She's here! Amaya is here!" He jumped up and down and ran wildly throughout the house.

Jaden dashed to get his bin of race cars. He wanted to show them to Amaya.

"Here, Amaya, you can have this red one," Jaden said.

Daddy laughed. "She won't be able to hold the car yet, champ. It may be a while before she can play race cars with you."

Jaden was a little disappointed—he did not quite understand. He went to put the cars away and returned with a box full of building blocks.

"Come on, Amaya! Let's build a super-tall tower."

Jaden dumped the building blocks onto the floor. He wanted Amaya to come and play with him, but she didn't move.

"Why doesn't the baby want to play with me?" Jaden asked.

"Oh, honey," Mommy replied. "Amaya will love playing with you when she is a little bigger. At this age, babies eat and sleep, and then they eat and sleep some more. Do you want to know what you can do, though?

Jaden was happy to know that there was something he could do because he was beginning to feel sad.

"Yes, Mommy. Please tell me," said Jaden.

"Let's make a list. Number one, you can read to her. Babies love books."

Before Mommy could get to number two, Jaden ran to get his favorite books. He came back with a book about trucks and another one about animals.

"These books are great, but before you begin reading, let's talk about other things you can do with your baby sister," Mommy continued.

"You can sing, dance, and play peek-a-boo."

"Yay! I love dancing!" exclaimed Jaden.

"You can even hold her when Mommy and Daddy are watching, but always remember, safety first."

Jaden repeated, "Yes, safety first!"

"We will need to be very gentle with our new baby. She is so little, and not as strong as her big brother," explained Mommy.

Mommy smiled and placed Amaya safely into Jaden's arms.

Jaden held her close to his heart. "One day, you'll be strong like me, and we will build big, tall towers and climb into the treehouse together."

Jaden softly kissed his baby sister's forehead and whispered, "I'm happy to have you home."

Made in the USA
Columbia, SC
21 December 2020